ILLUMINATION PRESENTS

GRU'S GADGET GUIDE

LB kids

2017 © Universal Studios. Despicable Me 3 is a trademark and copyright of Universal Studios. Licensed by Universal Studios. All Rights Reserved. Cover design by Centrum Books LTD. Hachette Book Group supports the right to free expression and the value of copyright. The purpose of copyright is to encourage writers and artists to produce the creative works that enrich our culture. The scanning, uploading, and distribution of this book without permission is a theft of the author's intellectual property. If you would like permission to use material from the book (other than for review purposes), please contact permissions@hbgusa.com. Thank you for your support of the author's rights.

Little, Brown and Company • Hachette Book Group • 1290 Avenue of the Americas • New York, NY 10104 • Visit us at lb-kids.com • www.despicable.me • LB Kids is a division of Hachette Book Group, Inc. • The LB Kids name and logo are trademarks of Hachette Book Group, Inc. • The publisher is not responsible for websites (or their content) that are not owned by the publisher. • Published simultaneously in Great Britain by Centrum Books LTD. • First U.S. edition: May 2017 • Centrum Books LTD. • 20 Devon Square • Newton Abbot, Devon, TQ12 2HR, UK • books@centrumbooksltd.co.uk • ISBNs: 978-0-316-50773-8 (paperback), 978-0-316-47618-8 (Canadian edition), 978-0-316-50769-1 (ebook), 978-0-316-50770-7 (ebook), 978-0-316-50772-1 (ebook)

Printed in the United States of America

Do you know the best part of being a villain or a spy? Is it the fabulous outfits? Possibly. Is it the excitement? Well, that's good, too, but by far the greatest things about being a villain or a spy are the GADGETS!

Not only is having a gadget in your hand an easy way to make you look super-cool, but they can help you escape from a tight spot!

So, what are you waiting for? Read on and equip yourself with facts and stats on all the latest gadgets.

You also need a bit of luck.

I look super-cool without a gadget in my hand, too.

This book says it's the most comprehensive guide ever compiled, but did it include the firsthand experience of the greatest villain-turned-spy of all time? It did not! So keep an eye out for notes throughout the book by me, Gru, who has used and helped create most of these gadgets.

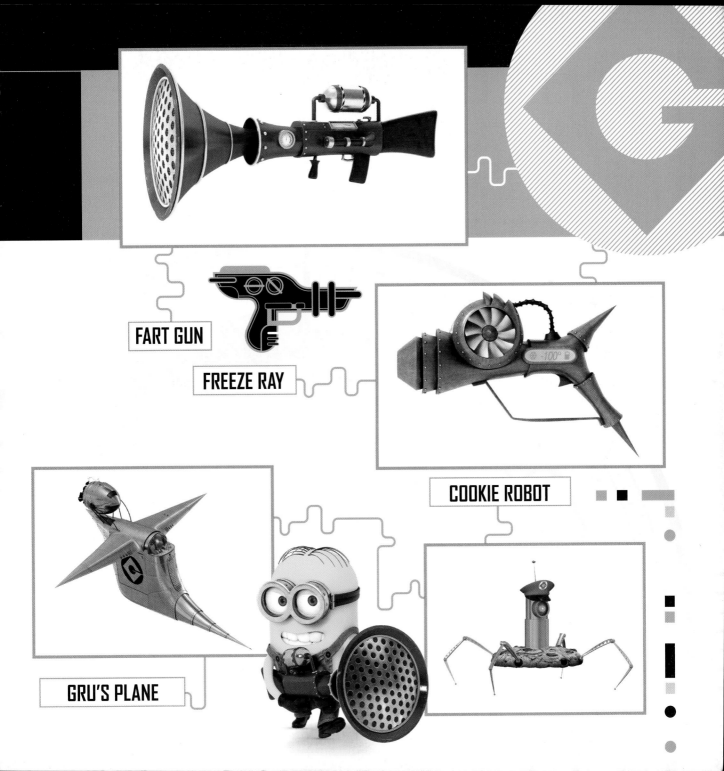

FART GUN

FREEZE RAY

COOKIE ROBOT

GRU'S PLANE

FELONIUS GRU

Never in the history of villainy and espionage has a single person's career path been as back-and-forth from villain to spy . . . and back again, as Gru's.

He is widely credited with pulling off the greatest criminal heist ever when he shrunk and stole the moon, *and* also with saving the world from El Macho's unstoppable PX-41 Minion army.

Gru is also now a father and husband—so you might imagine there is never a dull moment in the Gru household. Let's learn more about him.

There is no proof that I did this. But also, after I did this, I put it back!

I'm never credited for the time I was a legitimate businessman, making delicious jams and jellies.

NAME:	Felonius Gru
OCCUPATION:	Villain (former) AVL spy
FAMILY:	Lucy Wilde (wife); Margo, Edith and Agnes (daughters); his mom; Dru (twin brother)
MOST LIKELY TO SAY:	"Assemble the Minions!"

FREEZE RAY

*It's cooled down some **very hot** situations. It's particularly useful when you want to shorten a coffee shop line.*

The Freeze Ray is one of Gru's favorite gadgets.

It was invented by Dr. Nefario, who first showcased it at Villain Con in 1968— and first used soon afterward during the mysterious disappearance of the Queen of England's crown. ←

A young boy's first heist in a distinguished career of villainy.

ICE BEAM COMES OUT HERE

NOT effective against Flame Throwers

POWER TURBINE

◀━━━━ ⋯⋯ POINT THIS WAY

(G)
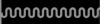

TEMPERATURE GAUGE

HOW IT WORKS

This gadget projects
a ray that freezes
anything instantly.

*IMPORTANT NOTE: The ice
produced is very brittle and
will smash on impact.*

BATTERY CHARGE INDICATOR

❄ **-100°** 🔋

TRIGGER

*Announce gadget
name after pressing*

HOLD HERE

* DON'T leave
unattended near
the girls.

GRU'S PLANE

A distinctive and awesome plane is an essential piece of tech for any aspiring super villain or spy.

You'll notice that Gru's plane has all the distinctive hallmarks of a Gru vehicle: the odd shape, silver color, and of course the *G* logo (branding is key to any enterprise for a villain or a spy).

Every good plane starts out as a simple collection of ideas on a blueprint.

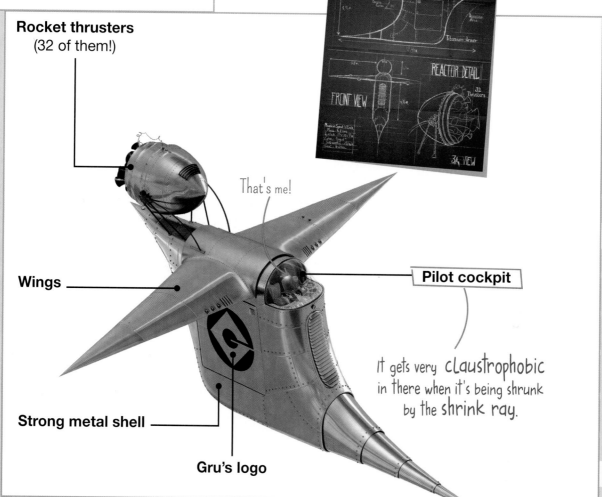

Rocket thrusters
(32 of them!)

That's me!

Wings

Pilot cockpit

It gets very **claustrophobic** in there when it's being shrunk by the **shrink ray.**

Strong metal shell

Gru's logo

MY HEIST PLANE
SIDE VIEW
FRONT VIEW
REACTOR DETAIL
32 Thrusters
3/4 VIEW

And if the plane ever did come under attack from an unfriendly plane, it could defend itself like this:

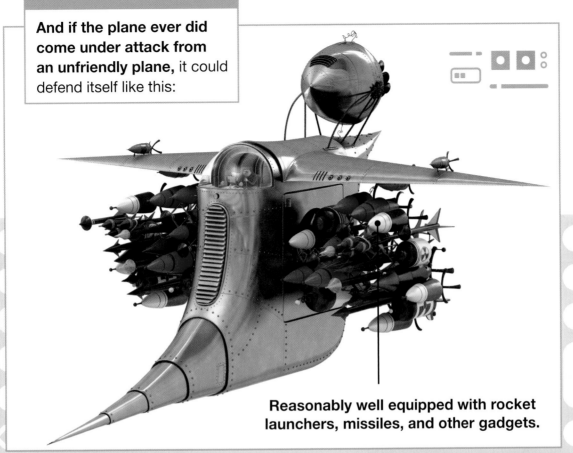

Reasonably well equipped with rocket launchers, missiles, and other gadgets.

Someone's
~~GRU'S~~ LAIR

Whoever's Lair this is, they're obviously **very** cool and handsome.

A villain's or spy's lair is the place where they can develop gadgets and hatch plans to destroy/save the world in secret.

There's nothing that ruins a perfectly good plan more quickly than prying eyes snooping into what you're doing—so keeping the lair secret is top priority.

It's important for a lair to have space and functions to cover lots of different plans, including:

A big stage from which to deliver grand plans or pep talks to your employees/Minions.

Mission control for rocket launches.

A yoga studio—a relaxed mind is a productive mind!

A lab in which you can create new gadgets.

ASSEMBLE THE MINIONS!

If you're looking for an army to help you go through and complete all your top-secret plans, then a Minion army is the only one you'll need.

Minions are unusual . . . creatures. If you've ever wondered what the anatomy of a Minion is like, then wonder no more and look at the blueprint below.

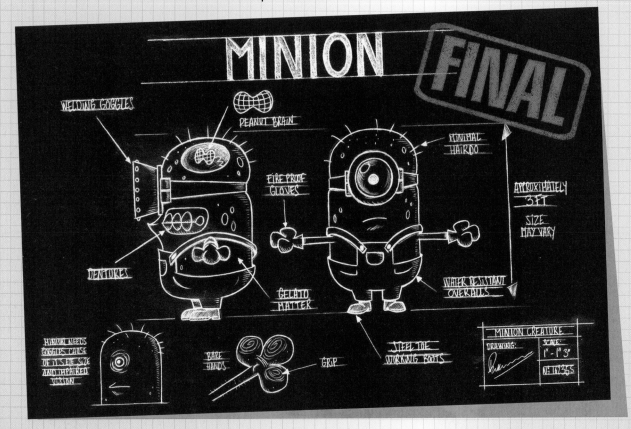

The Minions have all sorts of names—like Bob, Carl, and Tim.

But some have other names, too....
Let's meet some of the army.

Mel

You'll recognize Mel by his grumpy face, one eye, and his distinct hair: bald on top, hair around the sides!

Mel leads the Minions' revolt when they decide that they miss being evil and want to find a new master with more villainous ways.

The two MOST LOYAL Minions in the bunch!

DISLOYAL Minion who couldn't last on his own for five minutes!

Dave and Jerry

These two often travel as a pair, but it's easy to tell them apart. Jerry has spiky hair, whereas Dave's is parted in the middle.

They accompany Gru to Freedonia, and spend a lot of time with Edith tormenting Dru's butler.

FART GUN

The idea of this hilarious, amazing, and perhaps slightly pointless gadget was born from a simple mishearing.

Have you ever noticed how "dart" sounds very similar to "fart"? Well, from that, the Fart Gun was born, with the ability to seriously stink up a room.

Dr. Nefario did use the Fart Gun to knock out a PX-41 EL Macho...the stinkiest defeat EVER!

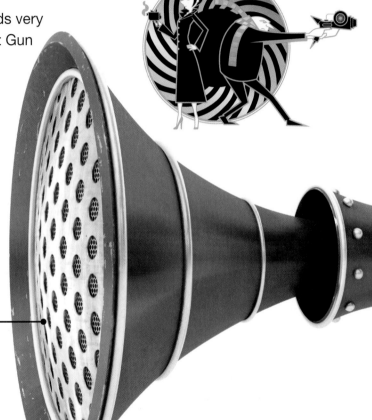

A 21-fart-gun salute is the highest honor.

Fart comes out here

Make sure you aren't downwind.

Pressure gauge

Gas canister

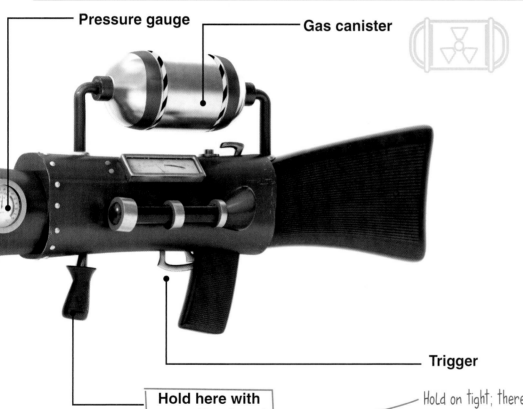

Trigger

Hold here with your other hand

Hold on tight; there's always some serious recoil.

FIRST appears in **DESPICABLE ME**

FACT FILE:

DR. NEFARIO

Dr. Nefario is Gru's gadget guru, as well as his most loyal friend.

Dr. Nefario has always considered Gru one of the greats of the super-villain world . . . and perhaps the spy world, too.

REAL NAME: Joseph Albert Nefario

NOTABLE INVENTIONS:
Freeze Ray, Boogie Robots, Cookie Robots, Fart Gun, Rocket, Gru's car and plane

SCIENTIFIC DISCOVERIES:
The Nefario principle

LESS NOTABLE INVENTIONS:
All-berry flavored jam

Unfortunately, due to unknown circumstances, Dr. Nefario is currently frozen in carbonite. The Minions are trying to figure out a way to unfreeze him.

It's not known how old **Dr. Nefario is . . .** but it has been suggested (although not scientifically proven) that you can tell how old someone is from the size of their ears, since the ears continue to grow throughout someone's life. From the size of Dr. Nefario's ears, we can assume that he's reasonably old.

This and the fact that he mishears most things I say to him.

COOKIE ROBOTS

A wise man, who was a little hard of hearing, once said that the ideas for the best gadgets are born from misunderstanding. From the same ears and brain that misheard and created the Fart Gun came the Cookie Robots.

Oh wait, this isn't one of the gadgets that was misheard; that was Boogie Robots. It turns out to be an easy mistake to make.

These robots are disguised as cookies and can be delivered into an unsuspecting home via a cookie box.

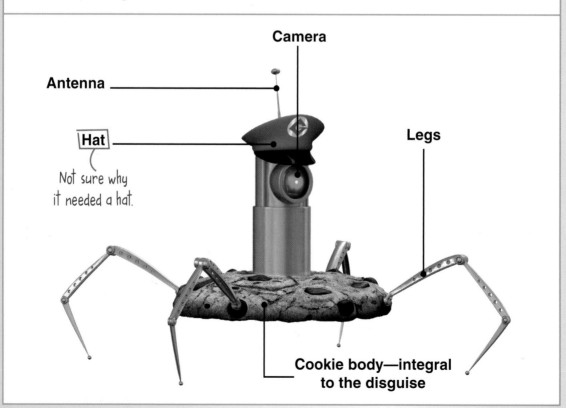

Camera

Antenna

Hat

Not sure why it needed a hat.

Legs

Cookie body—integral to the disguise

Stupid Vector; he had no idea these weren't **real** and **delicious** cookies!

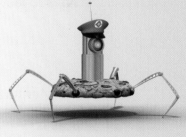

FIRST appears in *DESPICABLE* **ME3**

FACT FILE:

BALTHAZAR BRATT

He's the 80s-TV-star-turned-criminal-mastermind.

When his TV show *Evil Bratt* was canceled after he hit puberty, he vowed to seek revenge on the world that dared to cancel his show.

NAME:	Balthazar Bratt
GADGETS USED:	Self-Inflating Bubble Gum, Keytar, Disguises
VEHICLES:	Boat, Wingsuit, Wetsuit
OCCUPATION BEFORE VILLAINY:	Child TV Star
SIDEKICK:	Clive the Robot
EVIL PLAN:	Make a doomsday device to re-create the final episode of his TV show before it was canceled.
MOST LIKELY TO SAY:	"I've been a bad boy!" "Playing a villain on TV was fun—but being one in real life is better."

This guy's sense of style is *unbelievable*. IT HURTS MY EYES.

DRU'S VILLAIN CAR

When your dad's a super villain, it means he will hand down his awesome gadgets and vehicles to you.

Winch

This car is totally AWESOME!

Sound system

The wheels turn to the side and inflate so it can travel in water

Two seats

Nose can turn into a drill to tunnel the way out of danger

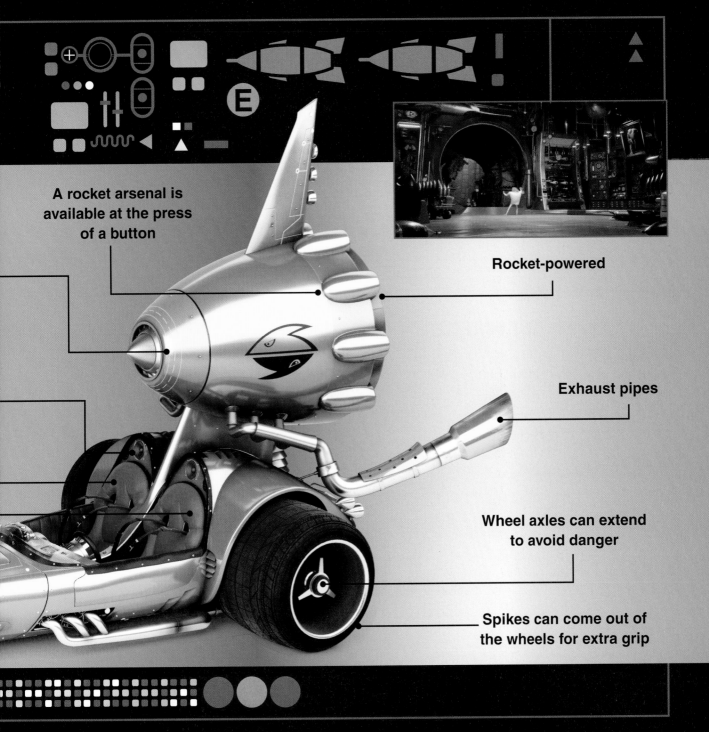

A rocket arsenal is available at the press of a button

Rocket-powered

Exhaust pipes

Wheel axles can extend to avoid danger

Spikes can come out of the wheels for extra grip

FIRST appears in DESPICABLE ME

THE GRUCYCLE

When you need to get somewhere in the nick of time and a rocket-powered car just won't do, the Grucycle is the vehicle for you.

EVERYONE must wear a helmet

Seats for two Minions

I look SO COOL and serious!

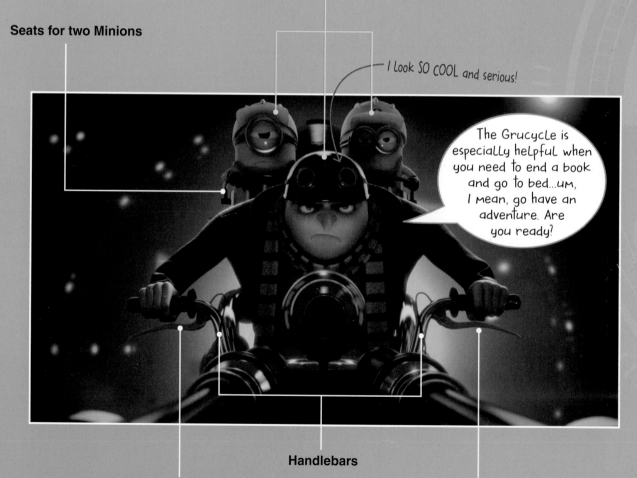

The Grucycle is especially helpful when you need to end a book and go to bed...um, I mean, go have an adventure. Are you ready?

Handlebars

Pull these to brake

Pull these to end story!